S0-AQC-494

DISCARDED

Property of
Nashville Public Library
615 Church St., Nashville, Tn. 37219

MEGATECH

Into Infinity

From Earth to the stars

David Jefferis

Crabtree
www.crabtreebooks.com

Introduction

Space is a dangerous place for humans. It is cold and difficult to live in. Earth is the only planet where humans can live without wearing spacesuits. So why do people want to explore space?

The answer seems to be "because it is there." The urge to explore space is the same one that makes people want to climb the highest mountain. Many people object to spending money on space exploration. They argue that the money would be better spent on Earth.

In fact, space exploration pays for itself many times over. Weather warnings, television, radio, and telephone links all depend on the use of satellites that are launched into space. These **satellites** will also help humans to someday extend exploration far beyond our **Moon**.

MEGATECH

Crabtree Publishing Company
PMB 16A,   612 Welland Avenue
350 Fifth Avenue   St Catharines
Suite 3308   Ontario, Canada
New York   L2M 5V6
NY 10118

Edited by
Isabella McIntyre
Coordinating editor
Ellen Rodger

Project Editor
Kate Calder
Assistant Editors
P. A. Finlay
Carrie Gleason
Production Coordinator
Rosie Gowsell
Technical consultant
Mat Irvine FBIS
Picture research by
Kay Rowley

Created and produced by
Alpha Communications in association
with Firecrest Books Ltd.

©2002 David Jefferis/Alpha
Communications

Cataloging-in-Publication Data
Jefferis, David.
    Into infinity: from earth to the
stars/ David Jefferis.
    p. cm. -- (Megatech)
    Includes index.
    ISBN 0-7787-0050-X (rlb) -- ISBN
0-7787-0060-7 (pbk)
    1. Astronautics--Juvenile literature.
2. Outer space--Exploration--Juvenile
literature. [1.Astronautics. 2. Outer
space--Exploration. 3. Space stations. 4.
Space vehicles.] I. Title. II. Series.
TL793.J42 2002
629.4--dc21
                    2001028704
                    LC

All rights reserved. No part of this
publication may be reproduced, stored
in any retrieval system or transmitted
in any form, by any means, electronic,
photographic, recording or otherwise,
except brief extracts for the purposes of
review, without the written permission
of the publisher and copyright holder.

Prepress
Embassy Graphics

Printed by
Worzalla Publishing Company

Previous page shows:
Laser-powered spacecraft near
the planet Jupiter.

Pictures on these pages,
clockwise from far left:
1   Future Moon base scene.
2   Design for a future
spacecraft, with rotating
sections to give crew a sensation
of weight during a voyage.
3   Earth's natural satellite,
the Moon.
4   Crew modules for a Mars base.
5   Advanced Shuttle, releasing a
satellite into orbit above Earth.

Contents

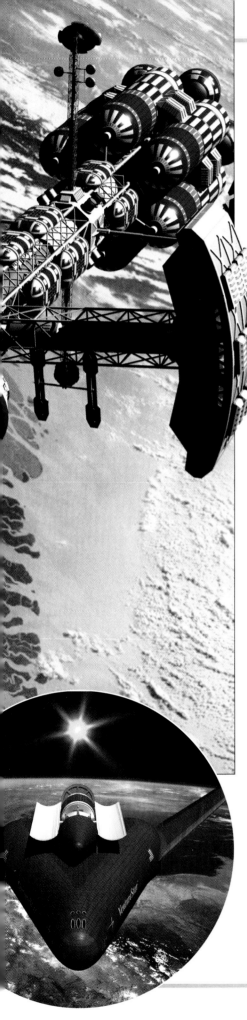

Our world in space

E arth is one of a group of planets that move around a **star** called the Sun. The Sun and its planets are called the **solar system**.

▲ *The Moon is Earth's nearest neighbor in space.*

The solar system is the Earth's "local space area," but distances between the Sun and the planets are great. The Earth circles, or orbits, the Sun at a distance of nearly 93 million miles (150 million km). Mercury and Venus are closer to the Sun, while the other planets are farther away. Pluto is the farthest planet from the Sun. Pluto is about 40 times farther away than Earth and is a frozen planet. The daytime temperature on Pluto is just -380°F (-230°C).

▲ *Earth is the only known planet where water flows freely. Scientists say that water is necessary for life to exist on a planet.*

A suit is tested to make sure the joints are flexible

▲ *A spacesuit is needed to survive in space or on other planets. So far, no one has found another planet with air that humans can breathe.*

W hen compared with Earth, the other **planets** are not comfortable to live on. They are either too hot or too cold, or have atmospheres that will not support life.

Far beyond the solar system are the stars. Many of these stars have planets. Even if there is no other planet like Earth in the solar system, there may be one circling another star.

??? How far away is the Moon?

The Moon is Earth's nearest neighbor in space – but it is still the farthest place that humans have reached. The Moon moves around the Earth in a nearly circular orbit, at a distance of about 240,000 miles (386,000 km).

When astronauts went to the Moon in the 1960s and 1970s, the trip took about three days. Astronaut Harrison Schmitt is shown inspecting a rock in this 1972 photo (right). Today, spacecraft such as the United States Space Shuttle and Russian Soyuz missions stay much closer to home. They orbit the Earth about 250 miles (400 km) up.

U.S. astronaut Harrison Schmitt on the Moon

Pluto has one moon, called Charon

Neptune has faint rings and eight moons

▶ *The planets of the solar system, lined up against a small part of the Sun. The big outer planets are many times larger than Earth.*

Uranus rotates on its side, like a top. It has seventeen moons

Saturn has large rings and 30 moons

▲ *The Sun is just one of more than 100 billion stars that swirl together in a huge group called the Milky Way galaxy. Many of these stars have planets. There are billions of other galaxies. If traveling to other galaxies ever becomes possible, future astronauts will have plenty of places to go!*

Jupiter is the biggest planet and has eighteen moons. The oval area known as the Great Red Spot is a raging storm big enough to swallow Earth

Mars has two tiny moons, called Phobos and Deimos

Earth and Moon

Venus

Mercury

Sun

Leaving planet Earth

The only way humans can travel into space is by using powerful rockets. The first rocket to travel into space took off in 1957. Today, different types of spacecraft are launched every week.

To fly safely into orbit, a spacecraft has to reach a speed of nearly five miles per second (7.8 km/sec). If it is any slower it will fall back to Earth. There were no rockets powerful enough for this until the late 1950s, when Russia and the United States raced to send the first rocket into space. The Russians sent the world's first artificial satellite, called *Sputnik 1*, into orbit in 1957. A satellite is an object that travels around a large body in space. A few years later, the United States took the lead in space exploration. In 1969, American astronauts landed on the Moon.

▲ *The United States Saturn V launched missions to the Moon in the 1960s and 1970s. The Saturn V remains the biggest space rocket ever made. It was 363 ft (111 m) tall, and weighed over 3000 tons when fully fueled.*

There are different kinds of rocket launchers, but they all work in a similar way. Rocket motors use a mixture of fuel (often liquid hydrogen) and an oxidizer (liquid oxygen), which is needed to allow the fuel to burn. The super-hot gases rush out of the back of the rocket with great force which causes it to blast off.

Rocket boosters fall away into the sea when their fuel is used

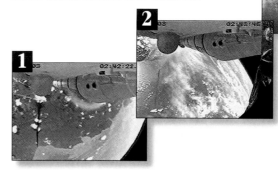

1 **2** **3**

◀▲ *These pictures were taken by onboard cameras during a launch. You can see one of the boosters falling away in picture 3.*

A spacecraft has several different detachable parts that help to launch it into space. To reach orbital speed, rockets need several booster stages to build up speed gradually. As each booster stage uses up its fuel, the booster falls away and the next stage takes over. Most space launchers use three or four stages to reach orbit.

◀ *Most space cargoes are launched without astronauts on board. Extra rocket boosters clustered around the base of this rocket increase the weight it can carry into space.*

What is an orbit?

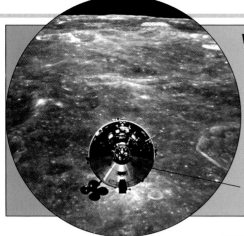

Apollo spacecraft orbiting the
Moon in 1970

An orbit is the curving path that an object in space takes to travel around another larger one. For example, the Moon is the Earth's natural satellite, completing one orbit around our planet every 27.3 days. As the Moon orbits, different parts of its surface are illuminated by the Sun, which is why it seems to change shape, from a round, full Moon to a slim crescent.

Spacecraft orbit around the Earth at various heights. Space shuttles stay fairly low, at about 250 miles (400 km). Many satellites may orbit much farther away at distances of up to 22,300 miles (35,880 km).

This Russian rocket is taken to the
launch pad along rail tracks

◄ This is an Ariane V rocket, which has a main center-body and two boosters used for takeoff. These drop away when their fuel is used up. Ariane does not carry people – its normal load is one big, or several smaller satellites. The rocket is not used again after a launch. The pieces fall into the Atlantic Ocean after use.

▲ Ariane rockets fly from Kourou,
a space base located in
South America.

Satellite revolution

▲ *The Hubble Space Telescope takes fantastic pictures of stars and planets.*

There are hundreds of satellites in orbit around the Earth. The biggest are the size of a large truck. The smallest may be no larger than a TV set.

▲ *Satellites orbit the Earth at various distances. Many circle our planet just a few hundred miles up. Others orbit much farther away.*

Many satellites take pictures of Earth from space. These satellites have many useful jobs, such as providing weather information. From orbit, cameras record storms and hurricanes as they form, giving warning to people here on Earth. Other dangers can also be spotted, such as forest fires, volcanic ash clouds, and shifts in earthquake zones. Icebergs can be tracked if they drift into shipping lanes.

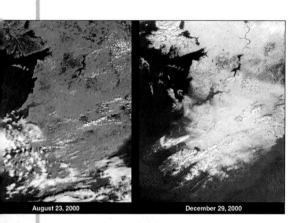

August 23, 2000   December 29, 2000

▲ *Ireland shown in the summer (left) and in the winter after a heavy snowfall.*

The calm center of a hurricane is called the eye

▲ *Some satellites can map earth movements to warn of an earthquake. This computerized image shows a part of California that has many earthquakes.*

▲ *Weather satellites can give warnings of bad weather to come. In this photo, a hurricane moves towards the east coast of the United States.*

Temperatures in these arched streams of hot gas may reach over a million degrees

◄ *The TRACE satellite has a telescope to study the Sun up close. In this image, huge loops of fire burst above the Sun's hot surface.*

◀ IRAS was an astronomy satellite that measured heat in the farthest parts of the universe.

How do satellites get their power supply?

The long "wings" you see in this picture provide a clue to this question. They are made of solar cells which are small squares of silicon material that have a very useful function – they turn the energy from sunlight into electricity. Satellites that regularly pass into the Earth's shadow use their solar cells to charge batteries for the dark periods. The biggest solar panels are used on the International Space Station (see pages 12-13). They provide power for the astronaut crew and their equipment. On space missions into the outer solar system, where the Sun's rays are weaker, other sources of power will be used.

◀ Russia's Sputnik 1 was the world's first satellite in 1957. It weighed about 184 lb (84 kg).

Communications satellites, or **comsats**, are used to send TV and radio signals around the world. A comsat picks up signals from a ground station, strengthens the signal, then relays it to another ground station. This station may be halfway around the world. The **Global Positioning System (GPS)** uses many small satellites to send signals to Earth. A hand-held GPS receiver can pinpoint your exact position anywhere on Earth.

Other satellites include the Hubble Space Telescope, which peers into the depths of space to produce spectacular pictures of stars and planets that help to map the universe.

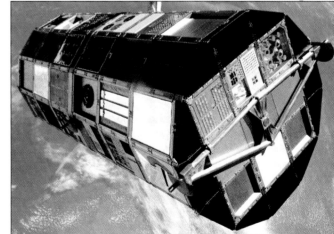

▲ The panels on this satellite were each made of a different material to test how they hold up in the harsh conditions of space.

9

Space trucking

The U.S. Space Shuttle was designed as a "space truck," to take big cargoes into space. It is also made to be partly reusable. The solid rocket boosters and the shuttle orbiter itself can be flown many times.

▲ The Space Shuttle is taken to the launch area on a massive crawler vehicle, which is also used as the launch pad.

At takeoff, a space shuttle consists of a winged orbiter attached to a huge external tank (ET) which supplies fuel to an orbiter's three main engines. On each side of the tank is a solid rocket booster (SRB). At takeoff, all five engines fire to send the craft into space.

▶ In space, the Shuttle Orbiter's doors stay open – they have built-in radiators to cool the spacecraft in the direct rays of the Sun.

Thruster jets at nose and tail

OMS engines for final thrust into and out of orbit

Flight deck

Cargo bay door

Load in cargo bay

Main engines

Slightly more than two minutes after takeoff, the SRBs drop away, as their fuel is used up. The orbiter carries on, using fuel from the ET. Soon the fuel is used up, and the ET is also dropped. Orbital maneuvering system (OMS) rockets in the Shuttle's tail give it the final push into orbit, at 17,270 mph (27,800 km/h). Fine maneuvers in space are made using thruster jets at the nose and the tail of the Shuttle.

▶ The Orbiter's flight deck has nine video screens that display important flight information. Other controls are fitted across the ceiling and center panel.

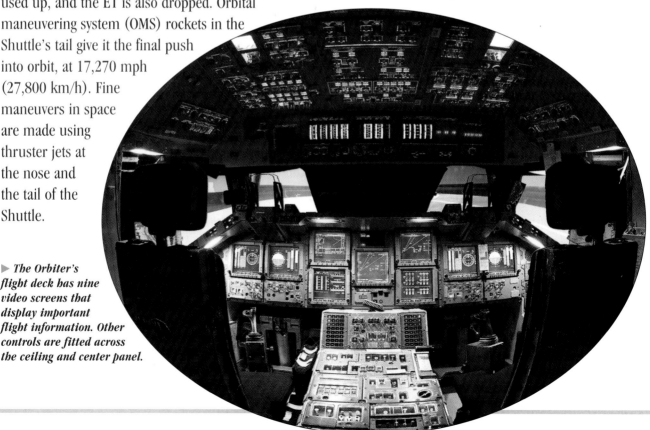

▲ Shuttle missions include taking satellites into space and repairing existing satellites. Here, an astronaut fits a new section to the International Space Station.

◀ At takeoff, five engines thrust together – two SRBs, plus the Orbiter's three main engines. The main engines get their fuel from the huge external tank.

A parachute is released from the Orbiter's tail section

Shuttle cargoes range from telescopes to space station sections, or modules. During a week in space, astronauts go outside the Shuttle on spacewalks to adjust or fix equipment. They wear spacesuits and propel themselves with jetpacks on their backs called Manned Maneuvering Units (MMUs).

When the Shuttle returns, the pilot maneuvers the Orbiter tail first and fires the OMS engines for 150 seconds to slow it down. The Orbiter turns around again and gradually loses height. It then hurtles through Earth's upper atmosphere, glowing with the heat of friction that reaches up to 3000°F (1648°C). Just 300 ft (91 m) above the ground, the landing gear is lowered and the Orbiter lands on a runway.

▲ On the runway, a parachute helps slow the Orbiter to walking pace. Most flights end in Florida, but for landings elsewhere, the Orbiter can be carried back on a 747 jet.

Living in space

▲ *An astronaut, shown above, helps attach a new Space Station module.*

Several space stations, including the U.S. Skylab in the 1970s and Russia's Mir, which stayed in orbit for fifteen years, have allowed astronauts to live in space for weeks, and even months at a time.

Today, the International Space Station, also called ISS or Alpha, is being put together in orbit and is made up of several modules, or parts. The modules are transported from Earth aboard U.S. Space Shuttles and Russian spacecraft, to be linked together in space. Astronauts make spacewalks to secure final connections. With every mission the ISS gets slightly larger – eventually it could have room for as many as seven people.

Some of the many jobs for astronauts on the ISS include maintaining the systems needed to provide power, light, and air. When the shuttle is in orbit, everything inside becomes weightless, including people! Keeping fit is very important because being weightless weakens the body. The ISS is bigger than earlier space stations, but still gets messy. Everything floats around unless it is tied down.

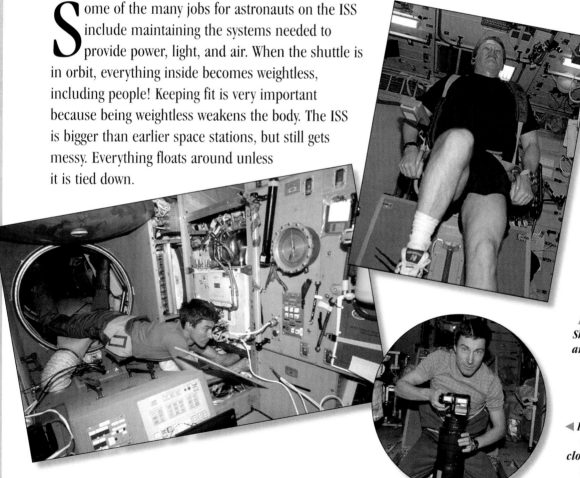

▲ *Astronaut William Shepherd works out on an ISS treadmill called an ergometer.*

◀ *Krikalev gets a camera ready to take some closeup pictures of Earth through a porthole.*

▲ *Russian cosmonaut and flight engineer Sergei Krikalev floats through a hatch to adjust ISS equipment.*

??? Is being weightless dangerous?

An object in orbit floats as if it is completely weightless. It is more accurate to describe this weightless state as free fall or microgravity. Astronauts feel only about one millionth the force of gravity that people feel on Earth.

For short periods, free fall is not dangerous, although many astronauts get space sickness, which makes them feel nauseous. Over a long time, muscles and bones lose their strength, and organs, such as the heart, become weak. Regular exercise is essential, but even so, cosmonaut Sergei Avdeyev, who spent many months aboard the Mir space station, returned to Earth too weak to throw a box of matches. It took him a year back on Earth to regain his full strength.

O ne problem that pioneers of space flight did not foresee is what to do with a space station when it is no longer needed. One solution is to **de-orbit** the craft, using braking rockets. Skylab and Mir returned to Earth this way, burning up as they hurtled into the upper atmosphere. Even so, some parts survived and hit the Earth. The ISS is by far the biggest man-made object in the sky, so getting rid of it may be a problem in the mid-21st century.

▲ *The ISS should look like this when finished. At top left is a Russian Soyuz spacecraft. A U.S. Shuttle is shown docked at the other end.*

▶ *By early 2001, the ISS had long solar panels fitted to provide electric power. A Soyuz spacecraft, shown right, is docked at the top end of the space station.*

Dangers of space

H umans have been traveling in space since 1961, yet leaving Earth is still a very risky adventure.

▲ The crew of the Apollo 13 Moon mission barely survived when equipment failed in flight.

Problems in space travel are caused by equipment failure or the natural hazards of space itself. Rockets have had mechanical failures, especially in the early days of space travel. In 1967, cosmonaut Vladimir Komarov became the first person to die in space, when his spacecraft failed on **re-entry**.

► Stars that are billions of years old may explode, throwing off a cloud of glowing dust and gas that flies through space.

► Astronauts have to perform all tasks perfectly so that equipment does not fail them in space. Here, an astronaut practices an assembly job in a special water tank, before leaving Earth.

O ther disasters have included launch pad fires and explosions. In 1986, the crew of the Space Shuttle *Challenger* died when the craft blew up shortly after liftoff.

Once in space, the dangers of any space flight are just starting. There is no air in space, so breathing systems inside the spacecraft have to be totally reliable. The hull has to be completely airtight to prevent any leaks.

◄ Despite safety measures, every space flight is risky. There have been several fatal accidents since humans first traveled into space.

► In space, the Sun's rays are deadly to an unprotected astronaut. This picture was taken by special instruments to show detail – the Sun is not really blue!

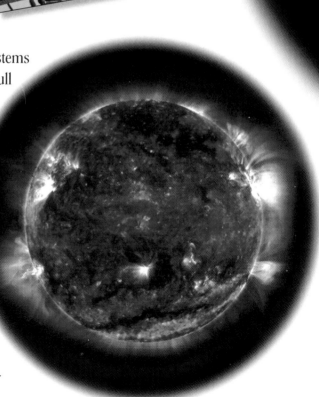

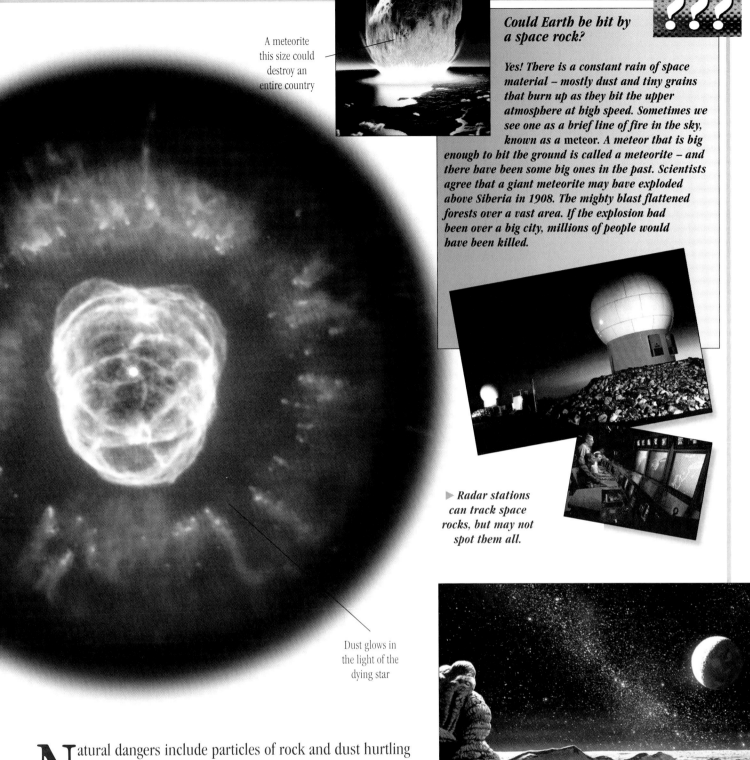

A meteorite this size could destroy an entire country

???

Could Earth be hit by a space rock?

Yes! There is a constant rain of space material – mostly dust and tiny grains that burn up as they hit the upper atmosphere at high speed. Sometimes we see one as a brief line of fire in the sky, known as a meteor. A meteor that is big enough to hit the ground is called a meteorite – and there have been some big ones in the past. Scientists agree that a giant meteorite may have exploded above Siberia in 1908. The mighty blast flattened forests over a vast area. If the explosion had been over a big city, millions of people would have been killed.

▶ *Radar stations can track space rocks, but may not spot them all.*

Dust glows in the light of the dying star

Natural dangers include particles of rock and dust hurtling through space. Even a tiny grain can pack a mighty punch, and at least one Shuttle Orbiter has had a flight-deck window scarred by the impact of a dust-sized piece of space rock.

The Sun enables life to exist, but many of its rays are deadly. On Earth, the atmosphere keeps us safe, but in space an unprotected astronaut can be caught in an invisible sea of **radiation**.

▲ *In the outer solar system, the Sun appears as little more than a bright star, and gives almost no heat. On Pluto, you would freeze hard as rock in a few seconds.*

15

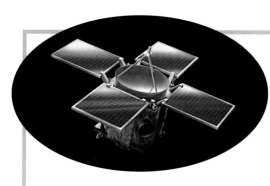

▲ The NEAR-Shoemaker probe spent much of 2000 very close to the asteroid Eros. It landed in early 2001.

Roving robots

Spacecraft sent to explore deep space are machines that are controlled by computer and built to survive missions that may last for many years. The space rock shown here, called Eros, is 196 million miles (316 million km) from Earth.

Eros is an **asteroid**. It is a remnant from billions of years ago, when the planets were being formed from loose bits of space debris swirling around the young Sun.

The spaceprobe NEAR-*Shoemaker* spent months in close orbit around Eros, taking photographs and finding out what it is made of. When these studies were finished, the probe was sent closer, to make the first landing on an asteroid.

Probe landed in this area

◀ NEAR-Shoemaker was launched into space in the nose-section of an uncrewed Delta rocket.

Eros is just 21 miles (34 km) long, with a shape like a shoe, or a peanut. Its year is longer than Earth's because it takes 1.76 years to circle the Sun. A day on Eros lasts just 5.27 hours. The tiny asteroid has little gravity – an object that weighs 100 lb (45 kg) on Earth would weigh only about one ounce (28 g) on Eros.

▲ Eros appears to change shape as it turns in the sunlight.

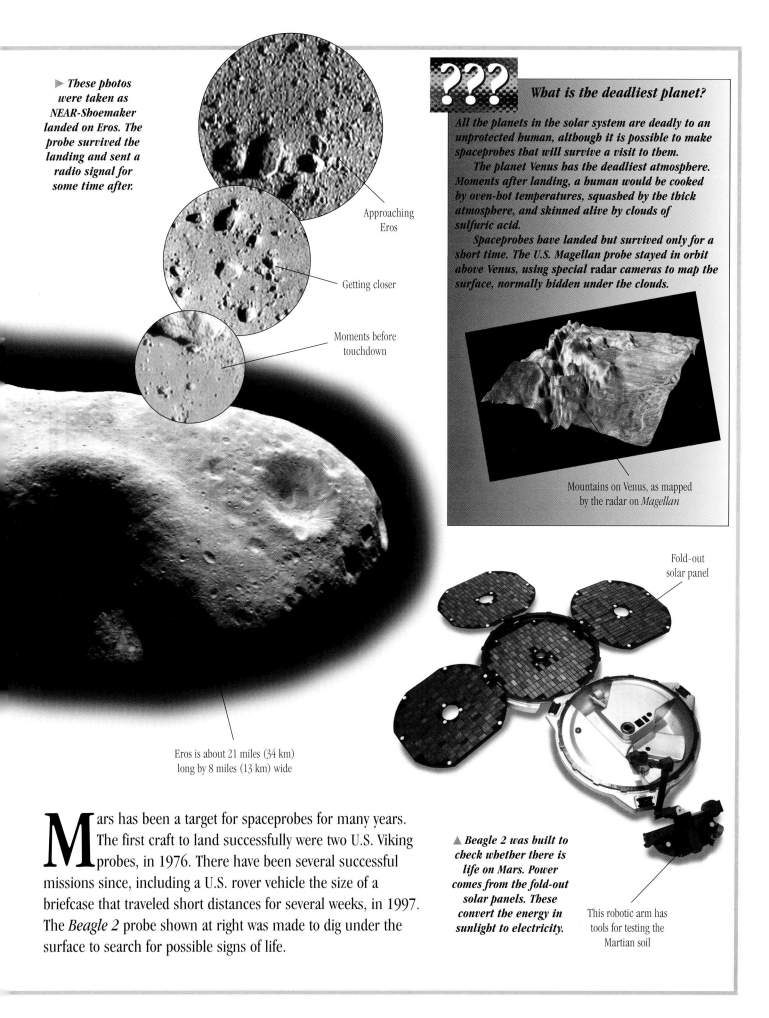

> ▶ *These photos were taken as NEAR-Shoemaker landed on Eros. The probe survived the landing and sent a radio signal for some time after.*

Approaching Eros

Getting closer

Moments before touchdown

Eros is about 21 miles (34 km) long by 8 miles (13 km) wide

??? What is the deadliest planet?

All the planets in the solar system are deadly to an unprotected human, although it is possible to make spaceprobes that will survive a visit to them.

The planet Venus has the deadliest atmosphere. Moments after landing, a human would be cooked by oven-hot temperatures, squashed by the thick atmosphere, and skinned alive by clouds of sulfuric acid.

Spaceprobes have landed but survived only for a short time. The U.S. Magellan probe stayed in orbit above Venus, using special radar cameras to map the surface, normally hidden under the clouds.

Mountains on Venus, as mapped by the radar on *Magellan*

Fold-out solar panel

Mars has been a target for spaceprobes for many years. The first craft to land successfully were two U.S. Viking probes, in 1976. There have been several successful missions since, including a U.S. rover vehicle the size of a briefcase that traveled short distances for several weeks, in 1997. The *Beagle 2* probe shown at right was made to dig under the surface to search for possible signs of life.

> ▲ *Beagle 2 was built to check whether there is life on Mars. Power comes from the fold-out solar panels. These convert the energy in sunlight to electricity.*

This robotic arm has tools for testing the Martian soil

Exploring the icy dark

The outer planets are beyond the reach of human space flight. Spaceprobes have been sent to visit these planets. These space probe missions take years to complete because of the great distances involved.

▲ *A spaceprobe like this may land on a comet one day.*

Orbiting far from the Sun are giant planets made mostly of gas – Jupiter, Saturn, Uranus, and Neptune. Each planet is big enough to swallow the Earth many times. They are so far away that it can take a spacecraft many years to reach them. Beyond these gas giant planets is Pluto, a tiny planet that has one moon, called Charon. So far, no space mission has been to Pluto.

▼ **Comets** *drift beyond the planets.*

Communicating with probes exploring the outer planets is very slow. Over these great distances, even radio seems to move at a snail's pace. Traveling at 186,000 miles per second (300,000 km/sec), a signal takes at least 35 minutes to reach even the nearest gas-giant, Jupiter, and the same time for a reply to get back to Earth.

▲ *There may be ice geysers on super-cold Triton, moon of the distant planet Neptune.*

A large parachute slows the *Huygens* probe as it falls towards the surface of Titan

▲ *The atmosphere of Saturn's moon Titan is thick and smoggy, so the view at the surface could look like this. The Huygens lander might find out in 2004.*

What are Saturn's rings?

All the "gas-giant" planets have rings, but none are as spectacular as those around Saturn. Saturn's rings are a wonder of the solar system.

Many scientists think the rings are made mostly of chunks of ice that vary in size from boulders and rocks, down to grains of dust.

When photographed by Voyager spaceprobes in the 1980s, scientists could hardly believe what they saw. Saturn's rings looked much like the grooves in an old-fashioned LP record. There was even a twisted ring that looked like braided hair.

The Cassini probe, named after a fifteenth-century astronomer who studied Saturn, should tell us more. It will be launched in 2004 and will dive under the rings for closeup photos, before it orbits.

Cassini carries a smaller spacecraft, the Huygens probe, named after a Dutch astronomer. Huygens will land on Titan, a moon 3200 miles (5150 km) across.

P lanets are not the only objects in the outer solar system. Countless comets, dirty snowballs of dust, rocks, and ice, fly through space. Scientists think these objects are rubble left over from the early days of the solar system. When a comet drifts near the Sun, some of its ice can **vaporize**, showing up in Earth's night sky as a misty tail.

In 1986, the *Giotto* spaceprobe flew near Halley's comet. Future probes may land on a comet's cold surface.

▶ *One of the most dramatic views in the solar system is Saturn's rings, viewed from Saturn's cloud tops. Seen closeup, they are even more spectacular, with braids, kinks, and strange shadowy bands, like the spokes of a wheel.*

Back to the Moon

Astronauts first landed on the Moon in 1969. There were six Moon landings in all, but no humans have gone back since 1972. Now, some people think it is time to explore the Moon again.

▲ *Astronauts first landed on the Moon in 1969, on the Apollo 11 mission.*

The **Apollo** Moon missions of the 1960s and 1970s were successful but very costly. The missions were made when being first to the Moon was more important than the cost. Today, making space travel affordable is the top priority, but Moon flights are still expensive. Future travel to the Moon could be possible with the International Space Station. There are sixteen nations involved in the ISS, and if the costs were split, many countries could join together to pay for future Moon trips.

Future moon missions may be made to build a Moon base where astronauts can stay for long periods of time. The Moon base could be an airtight dome. Some scientists believe it would be safer to bury the dome under a thick mound of Moon soil.

A base near the Moon's south pole could use water that is frozen in deep craters, where the Sun's rays cannot reach. Such a base would be cheaper to maintain, as the water would not need to be hauled all the way from Earth.

◄ *Earth and Moon, shown to the same scale. Our planet is 7927 miles (12,756 km) across, while the Moon is just 2160 miles (3476 km) wide.*

There are no official plans for a return to the Moon, but plenty of people are interested. Private organizations, such as the U.S. Artemis Society, have campaigned for future Moon landings. China has its own space program and may also have plans for Moon missions in the near future.

◄ *One day, a robotic roving vehicle may visit the site of the first human landing.*

▶ *People have had ideas for exploring the Moon for many years. This 1950s comic showed a big Moon base.*

Is the Moon a dangerous place?

Without proper protection, no human could survive on the surface of the Moon. The Moon has no air, so a spacesuit has to be worn at all times. Temperatures on the Moon are far more extreme than on Earth. During a lunar day, which is two weeks long, the temperature soars above 212°F (100°C). In the equally long nights, it is a chilly -238°F (-150°C).

Two views of a possible future Moon base

▼ *This illustration shows what a future Moon base could include:*
1   The entry tunnel has an outer hatch (at far left) and an inner spacesuit changing room.
2   A thick dome keeps air in, and gives protection from meteorites.

3   There are five living levels inside the dome. A storage area is at the bottom. This also includes air-making equipment, as well as heating and cooling units.
4   A supply craft leaves the base, heading for a station in Earth's orbit.

1 **2** **3** **4**

Mars base

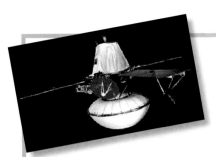

▲ *In 1976, two U.S. Viking probes were the first craft to test Mars for signs of life.*

One day, humans could travel to Mars. The trip would be a long one, with many dangers. Astronauts would land on a small planet, with a very thin atmosphere.

Human flight to Mars may be possible, but it will be far more difficult than a trip to the Moon. First, a cargo craft would be sent with the equipment needed by humans. When the basics for a base were safely on Mars, then a follow-up crewed ship could be sent.

Vehicle can travel at up to 20 mph (32 km/h)

▲ *In 2000, Australian Mars enthusiasts started to make a truck as a test-machine for a future two-person Mars rover.*

▲ *This design for a Mars base has a pair of two-floor cylinders that make a home for explorers from Earth. Entrance hatches are at the bottom of each cylinder.*

The flight to Mars would take several months. Cosmonaut Sergei Avdeyev showed in 2001 that humans can cope with flights that long – he stayed in space for a total of 748 days. Avdeyev thought that the isolation of a Mars trip could be boring and lonely, with only stars to look at out of the portholes. Mars astronauts would have a lot to keep them busy, including keeping life-support systems running safely!

Mars is mostly desert, but has an **ice cap** at each pole

Is there life on Mars?

The answer to this question is a strong "maybe," although life on Mars is probably no more than tiny micro-organisms.

The instruments on the two Viking probes of 1976 found no evidence of life. Since then, other probes have shown evidence that Mars once had surface water – and where there is water, there may be life.

In 1996, researchers claimed to find fossils of micro-organisms in a chunk of rock that had landed in Antarctica. Amazingly, this rock had been "splashed" off the red planet millions of years ago by a giant meteorite that crashed into Mars. In 2001, the researchers were sticking to their original claim, although not everyone agreed with them. We might have to go to Mars to find out for sure!

◀ *A busy day at a future Mars base. At bottom right, a geologist is shown looking at the fossil of an ancient Martian creature!*

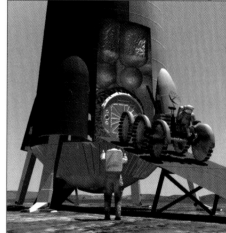

Once safely in Mars' orbit, astronauts would go down to the Martian surface in lander shuttles. Using the equipment already landed in the previous missions, the astronauts would be able to set up base for a long stay.

▲ *A Mars rover is driven carefully down a lander's ramp. Six wheels would allow the vehicle to travel over rocks and sand.*

After the base was set up, the landing team could explore. Spacesuits would be needed for walking, but Mars rovers would be designed to travel greater distances on the surface. Among the Martian sights to see would be the solar system's biggest volcano and the vast Marineris **rift valley**.

▶ *A robotic aircraft could fly over Mars, making a low-level map of the planet. This design has glider-like wings for flight in the thin air.*

▲ Explorers from Earth may come across strange lifeforms one day.

To the stars!

Humans have only explored space within our solar system. Some scientists think we could one day build spacecraft capable of traveling outside of our solar system.

▲ Future spacesuits may look much sleeker than today's bulky ones.

The problem with travel in deep space is the scale of the universe. Stars are so far apart that distances between them are measured in **light years** – how far light travels in a year at 186,000 miles a second (300,000 km/sec). The solar system's nearest star neighbor is Proxima Centauri, which is just over four light years away. That does not sound far but the farthest place humans have reached, the Moon, is less than two light *seconds* away!

▲ Starships have long been popular in sci-fi stories. This star truck dates from 1960.

Despite the distances involved, scientists have come up with possible solutions to the problems of traveling in deep space. One of these is known as a laser lightsail. This is a large sheet of thin plastic film, which spins to stay taut. A powerful laser on a "space lighthouse" is focused on the lightsail, and because pure light has a little pressure, the lightsail would slowly pick up enough speed to leave the solar system. Experts think a lightsail could take a tiny instrument package to Proxima Centauri in about 40 years.

The Planetary Society is a group that is experimenting with lightsails. The society plans to launch a design to prove the idea works.

Sails catch the light

Laser beam shown in red

Can a lightsail really work?

Lightsails are difficult to make. Some have been too heavy or have folded up at the wrong moment.

Some researchers think the idea has a great future. One plan calls for a lightsail that unfurls eight petals, to catch the sunlight. The tiny light pressure should enable the lightsail to increase speed.

The lightsail steers by adjusting the angle of its petals. Like a sailboat using wind, the lightsail rides sunlight across the sea of space. If experiments are successful, then a laser-powered version (shown at right) could be built.
This would be used for flights in deep space, where natural sunlight is too weak for propulsion.

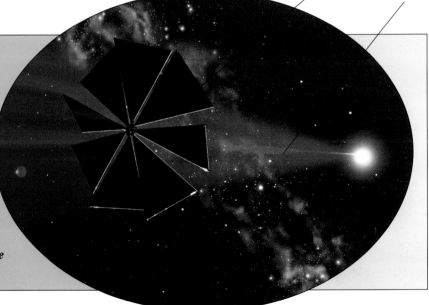

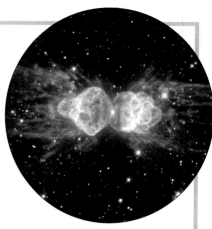

▲ We may find strange planets, even alien civilizations one day.

The fastest humans ever were the crew of *Apollo 10*, the second manned flight to the Moon, in 1969. They reached nearly 25,000 mph (40,250 km/h) returning to Earth. Even at this speed, it would take over 100,000 years to reach the nearest star! Without more speed, people on board will grow old and die before the journey is over. Scientists will have to develop technology for years to come before there is a breakthrough in space travel.

There might be progress, but building a starship is not possible yet, so the idea stays just a dream for now. Sending an instrument package on a lightsail explorer could be a future mission.

▲ Deep space and far stars will provide a gallery of fantastic sights for future travelers.

▶ One science-fiction theory is to make a starship by hollowing out an asteroid, and changing the inside into a space ark. The engines would use the mined-out material as fuel. Shuttles could enter and leave through a hatch at one end. Many generations of people would live and die on the asteroid ship before it reached the star system destination.

What's next?

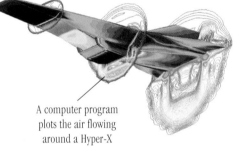

▲ In this Russian X Prize design, a small rocket takes off in mid-air from the back of a jet carrier plane.

We may travel to the stars one day, but in the near future, spacecraft will be traveling only inside the solar system.

Reliability and increased safety are the next targets for better space flight. An advanced Shuttle was planned for a first flight in 2010, but the project was put on hold. For now, the present U.S. Shuttles will stay in service, along with the Russian Soyuz and possibly a new Chinese crewed spacecraft.

◀ Hyper-X is a test model for very high-speed planes using new engines. Lessons learned from tests may lead to airplanes that fly on the edge of space.

Engines are placed under the belly

The International Space Station will be a base for scientific research. Traveling to the ISS is expensive, so developing cheaper space launchers will become very important. Space travel may cost a lot, but satellites will remain essential for **Earth resources** and communications.

A computer program plots the air flowing around a Hyper-X

◀ This future craft cruises over the volcanic moon Io, in orbit around the giant planet Jupiter. A laser beam from a space "power station" is used to heat onboard fuel. This then fires through the engine, to thrust the craft smoothly forward.

Will there be tourists in space?

The first person in space who was not a professional astronaut was a Japanese reporter, Toyohiro Akiyama. He visited the Russian Mir space station in 1990 and reported the visit on television. In 2001, Dennis Tito became the first real tourist, when he paid for a trip to the ISS. There are no official plans for more space tours, but the X Prize Foundation offers a prize of $10 million to the first team that sends a three-person craft to a height of more than 62 miles (100 km), and can do it again within two weeks. There is much interest in this, and many teams from around the world are taking part. Entries come from several countries, including Brazil, Britain, Canada, Russia, and the United States.

▶ This design is for a future "heavy lifter" shuttle, able to carry a massive load into space in one trip.

Booster engines are in this cluster of eight pods

Craft is designed to be fully reusable after each flight

S pace may become a battleground. So far, military satellites have been limited to cameras and other sensors, to keep watch on enemy troop movements. In the future, "space forts," armed with a powerful laser cannon, could be placed in orbit. These could shoot down enemy missiles moments after takeoff. The idea is to keep the peace, but many people think it would lead to an arms race in space.

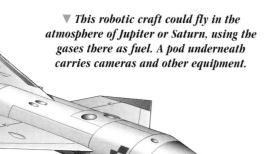

▼ This robotic craft could fly in the atmosphere of Jupiter or Saturn, using the gases there as fuel. A pod underneath carries cameras and other equipment.

▲ Laser cannons like this may be placed in orbit to zap enemy missiles in flight, before they can hit their target.

Time track

▲ *The first American astronauts were called the Mercury Seven.*

Spaceflight is only about half a century old, but progress has been rapid during that time. Humans have been to the Moon and may go much farther in the future.

1957   *Sputnik 1* is launched from Tyuratam cosmodrome on October 4. It is the world's first artificial satellite.

1957   A dog called Laika is sent into space aboard the Russian *Sputnik 2*.

1958   First U.S. satellite is launched, called *Explorer 1*. The carrier rocket is a four-stage *Juno 1*.

1960   First weather satellite is launched, called *Tiros 1*.

1960   First navigation satellite is launched, called *Transit 1B*.

▼ *Skylab was based on an empty fuel tank, which was fitted with science equipment, solar panels, and living quarters for the astronauts.*

1960   First spy satellite is launched. *Midas 2* is designed to spot the rocket heat from a missile launch.

1961   Russian cosmonaut Yuri Gagarin is the first human to orbit Earth.

1962   John Glenn is the first U.S. astronaut to orbit the Earth. He does it in a one-man Mercury spacecraft.

▲ *Shuttle Orbiters are flown back to base on a 747 jet.*

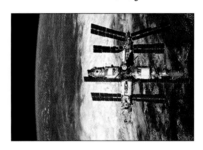

▲ *The Russian Mir space station stayed in orbit for 15 years.*

1962   *Telstar TV* satellite is launched. It provides live broadcasts for the first time between the U.S. and Europe.

1964   *Syncom 3* satellite is launched to broadcast sports at the Tokyo Olympic Games around the world.

1966   Russian *Luna 9* makes first successful landing on the Moon.

1969   Apollo 11 mission lands on the Moon. Neil Armstrong is the first human to set foot on the Moon. The TV broadcast is watched by an estimated 600 million people across the world.

1970   Japan becomes the fourth country to put a satellite into space.

1971   Russians launch their first space station, the *Salyut*.

1972   ERTS satellite is launched. It is the first Earth resources satellite, later renamed *Landsat*.

1973   Skylab 1 space station is put in orbit. Stays in space for six years.

1974   First education satellite is launched. ATS-6 beams learning TV shows to U.S. and, later, to 5000 villages in India.

1976   First *Viking* spaceprobe arrives in Mars orbit in June. Joined in August by *Viking 2*. Both probes release a lander to search for signs of life on Mars.

1979   First flight of the European Ariane space launcher, from a new space base built at Kourou in French Guiana, South America.

1981   First Space Shuttle flight. Shuttle *Columbia* flies 36 orbits, then glides back to a runway landing on Earth.

1981   *Venera 13* is launched by Russians to study the planet Venus.

1983   IRAS satellite is launched. Has an infra-red instrument that can detect very faint heat sources at the far reaches of the universe.

1984   First recovery of a satellite in space. *Palapa B2* and *Westar VI* satellites are taken back to Earth by Space Shuttle for repair and later reuse.

1986   The Space Shuttle *Challenger* explodes shortly after takeoff. The seven astronauts on board are killed.

1986   Approximately 3,465 spacecraft have been launched since 1957. There are 1,603 craft in space, most of them in Earth's orbit, plus 4,420 bits of debris such as booster casings.

▶ *A design for a crewed Mars spacecraft, shown leaving Earth's orbit.*

▶ *The International Space Station in early 2001.*

1986   The Russian space station Mir is launched. Designed for a five-year life, it continues in orbit for many years. It is finally sent back to Earth in 2001.

1990   Hubble Space Telescope (HST) is placed in Earth's orbit. It is the size of a big truck. More than ten years after its launch it still takes spectacular pictures. Occasionally, it needs repairs and updates. These are carried out in orbit by visiting Shuttle astronauts.

▲ *The Hubble Space Telescope was launched in 1990. Here it shows the planet Saturn.*

1993   A fleck of paint from a rocket casing hits a Shuttle Orbiter window. The collision speed is about 37 miles per second (60 km/sec), fast enough to crack the outer glass. Some experts believe that Earth will have its own ring in the future, made of bits of spacecraft.

1995   The *Galileo* spacecraft sends a probe into the atmosphere of the giant planet Jupiter. The probe returns useful information before it is crushed by Jupiter's atmosphere.

1996   U.S. astronaut Shannon Lucid makes the longest space flight by a woman, when she spends 188 days on board the Mir space station.

1997   The *U.S. Pathfinder* spacecraft lands on Mars. A small rover vehicle, controlled from Earth, explores the surrounding area for nearly three months before its batteries fail.

2000   The first crew goes aboard the International Space Station.

2001   The NEAR-*Shoemaker* space-probe lands on the asteroid Eros after a long investigation from nearby in space.

2001   60-year old Dennis Tito becomes a space tourist when he visits the International Space Station.

Into the future
2002   China plans to launch its first astronauts into Earth's orbit.

2004   Cassini spaceprobe explores the planet Saturn and its moons, and also launches a probe to the moon Titan.

2010   Chinese astronauts land on the Moon, beginning a new space race.

2015   Moon base is established.

2050   Humans land on Mars as part of an international exploration mission.

2100   First laser lightsail star probe launched, to the nearby **Alpha Centauri** triple-star system.

◀ *A Shuttle of the year 2020 may be fully automated. Here a satellite is released from a cargo pod fitted on top.*

Glossary

A n explanation of the technical terms and concepts in this book.

Alpha Centauri
The nearest star system to our solar system, just over four light years away. It consists of three stars – Alpha, Beta and Proxima Centauri. At least one planet orbits the red dwarf Proxima.

Apollo
The name given to the U.S. Moon-landing program of the 1960s and 1970s. The main spacecraft was a giant *Saturn V* booster. A two-man lander took astronauts to the Moon's surface. A three-man command module was all that finally came back to Earth.

Asteroid
A "minor planet," one of thousands. The biggest is called Ceres, and is about 620 miles (1000 km) across. The biggest asteroids are round, like micro-planets. Smaller ones, such as Eros, come in irregular shapes.

Atmosphere
The blanket of air that surrounds the Earth. Other planets often have atmospheres too – but in the solar system, none are breathable by humans.

Booster
A rocket attached to a main spacecraft to give extra thrust. The Space Shuttle has two solid rocket boosters, or SRBs.

Comet
Comets are often called "dirty snowballs," typically made of frozen ice, dust, and rock. If a comet passes near the Sun, its heat vaporizes some of the ice, which stretches out as a misty, glowing tail. This may stretch millions of miles, yet the material is so thin that it could fit into a medium-size suitcase.

Comsat
Short for communications satellite, which is used to beam radio and TV signals around the world.

De-orbit
To slow down a spacecraft, in order to re-enter the atmosphere.

◀ *A powerful laser being checked and tested as the main weapon of a space-based missile system.*

▲ *New spacecraft designs are tested in model form before the real thing is assembled.*

Earth resources
Type of satellite used to check on our planet. Weather, pollution, and crop growth are typical observations.

Fossil
Hardened remains of any plant or animal life from an earlier time – usually millions of years old.

Fuel cell
A device that mixes hydrogen and oxygen to make electricity. It is used for power aboard the Space Shuttle.

Galaxy
A vast group of stars, turning slowly in space. They come in various shapes and sizes – spiral, barred, irregular, and so on. A typical galaxy, such as our own Milky Way galaxy, may contain about 100 billion stars and is about 100,000 light years across.

Geyser
On Earth, a geyser is a spring from which boiling water or steam gushes out from time to time. On other planets, there may be geysers of different gases and liquids.

GPS
Global Positioning System. A group of satellites that beams signals down to Earth. A GPS receiver detects these signals and can work out its position precisely.

Gravity
Force of attraction between objects. Massive objects have a stronger gravity pull than less massive ones. Microgravity is in places where there is almost no gravity at all. On the International Space Station, microgravity is about a million times weaker than on Earth.

Hurricane
A violent tropical storm, usually with strong winds and heavy rains. Hurricanes are spiral shape and rotate around a central "eye," the calm center of the storm.

Ice cap
Area around the poles of a planet where ice forms. Earth and Mars have them. Earth's ice caps are frozen water, those of Mars are mostly frozen carbon dioxide gas.

Laser
An intense beam of light whose rays do not spread out quickly, like those of an ordinary light source, such as a flashlight. The letters in the word "laser" stand for light amplification by stimulated emission of radiation.

A lightsail is a possible design for a future spacecraft that is blown through space by light rays, much as a sailing ship uses the wind for propulsion.

Light year
The distance traveled by light in a year at a speed of 186,000 miles (300,000 km) per second. It is about 5.9 million million miles (9.5 million million km). Shorter distances may be measured in light hours, light minutes, or light seconds.

Meteor
Chunk of space rock or stone that burns up as it hits the Earth's upper atmsophere. If it survives to actually hit the ground it is called a meteorite.

Microgravity
See gravity.

Micro-organism
A living thing that is too small to be seen by the human eye – a microscope is used to view it.

Moon
Smaller companion to a planet. Earth's Moon is a cratered sphere 2,160 miles (3,476 km) across. Mars has two small lumpy moons, Phobos and Deimos, only a few miles across. The giant outer planets each have many more moons.

Near-Earth space
Orbital space around the Earth, nearer than the Moon. Space between the Earth and Moon is called cisluna space.

Orbit
The curving path one space body takes around another. A spacecraft in low orbit circles the Earth about every 80 minutes. The Moon orbits the Earth once every 27.3 days. The Earth and the Moon together orbit the Sun once a year, or every 365.3 days.

Planet
A large body in space which circles the Sun, or another star. The solar system's planets fall into two main types. The small and rocky planets are Mercury, Venus, Earth, and Mars. The bigger planets, made mostly of gases ("gas giants") are Jupiter, Saturn, Uranus, and Neptune. Tiny Pluto may be no more than a large asteroid.

Radar
System that transmits a radio beam. A solid object reflects some of this back to the transmitter. The reflection can be displayed on a TV screen as a glowing blob, which shows size, position, and distance.

Radiation
The range of wave energy found in nature. Radio waves and gamma rays are two extremes. Visible light is just a tiny part.

Rift valley
Valley formed when a section of land collapses between two other areas.

Re-entry
When a spacecraft comes back into the Earth's atmosphere.

Satellite
A body, either natural or human-made, that orbits a planet. The Moon is Earth's only natural satellite, but some other planets have more – Saturn has 28!

Solar panel
A flat piece of silicon material which is able to convert the energy in sunlight to electricity. They are often used to power satellites, when such panels are made into "wings" carrying hundreds or thousands of individual solar cells.

Solar system
The Sun, together with the planets, moons, comets, rocks, dust, and other debris that circle it. Other systems of planets and stars are known to exist, although a world like Earth has yet to be discovered.

Spacewalk
Another word for EVA or extra vehicular activity. It is when astronauts put on spacesuits and work in space.

Star
A glowing ball of gas in space. The nearest star to Earth is the Sun. The nearest other star is Proxima Centauri.

Vaporize
Frozen ice turning into a vapor or gas.

Year
The time it takes for a planet or moon to complete one orbit around the Sun. A day is the time is takes for Earth to rotate once around its own axis. Earth's day is just under 24 hours. The Moon has days and nights that last two weeks each.

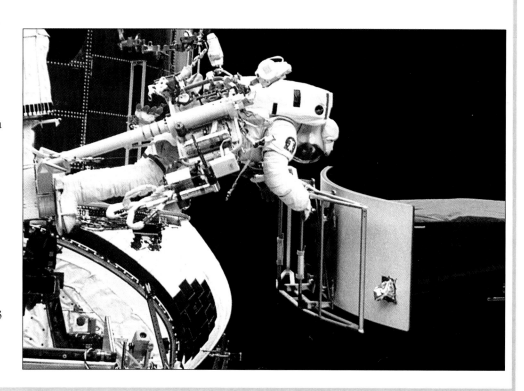

▲ This satellite has three solar panels that flip into position when the craft is in space.

▼ A Shuttle astronaut works just outside the cargo bay during an EVA or spacewalk.

Index

Acknowledgements
We wish to thank all those individuals and
organizations that have helped create this
publication.
Photographs were supplied by:
Alpha Archive
Arianespace
Artemis Society International
Beagle 2.com
Boeing Corporation
Don Davis
ESA European Space Agency
Goddard Space Flight Center
David Jefferis
JPL Jet Propulsion Laboratory
Lockheed Martin Corporation
LunaCorps
Marsupial/marsociety.org.au
NASA Space Agency
Orbital Sciences Corporation
Pat Rawlings/NASA
Planetary Society
US Air Force
X Prize Foundation

Digital art created by:
Rory McLeish
Gavin Page